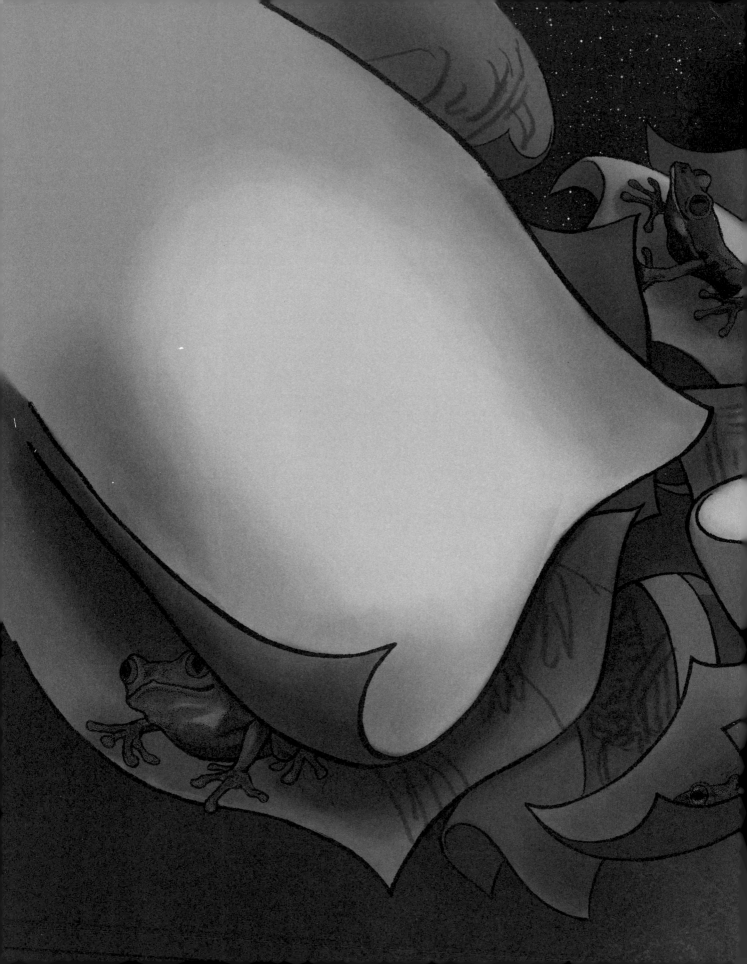

Sammy
EXPERIENCES
GOD

B&H
KIDS
Nashville, Tennessee

Written by Tom Blackaby *and* Rick Osborne

Illustrated by Isabella Kung

ISBN: 978-1-4336-7980-3
Dewey Decimal Classification: C231
Subject Heading: God \ Samuel, Judge

Printed in Malaysia
1 2 3 4 5 6 7 8 - 17 16 15 14 13

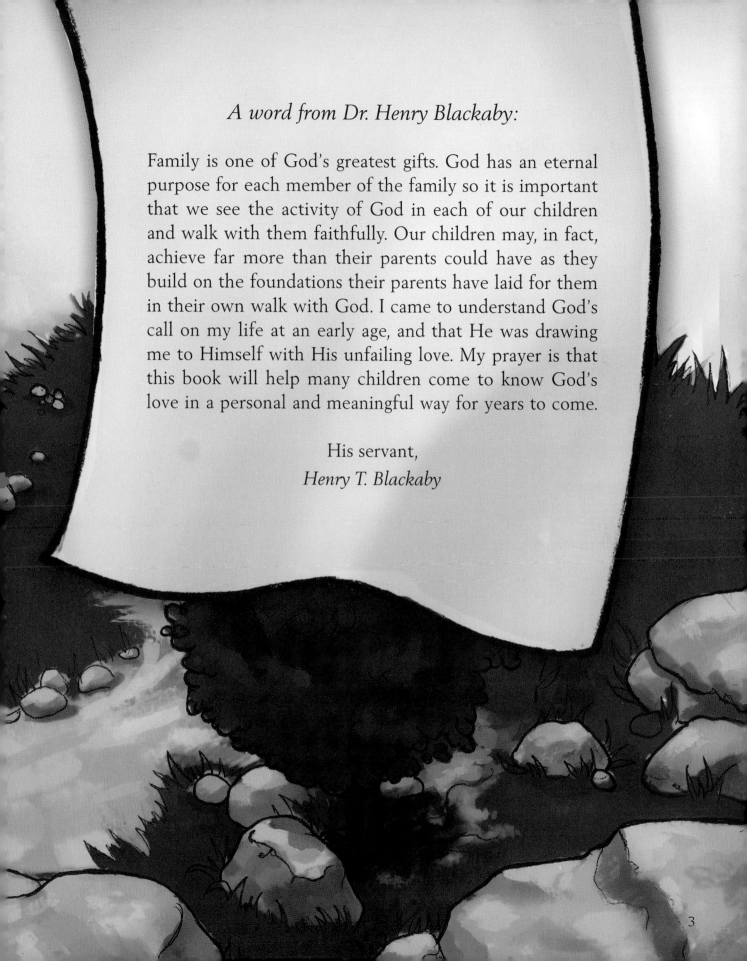

A word from Dr. Henry Blackaby:

Family is one of God's greatest gifts. God has an eternal purpose for each member of the family so it is important that we see the activity of God in each of our children and walk with them faithfully. Our children may, in fact, achieve far more than their parents could have as they build on the foundations their parents have laid for them in their own walk with God. I came to understand God's call on my life at an early age, and that He was drawing me to Himself with His unfailing love. My prayer is that this book will help many children come to know God's love in a personal and meaningful way for years to come.

His servant,
Henry T. Blackaby

One night, just like every other night, Sammy and his dad settled in to read.

Sammy sat wide-eyed, sketchpad in hand, as his father read story after story about God. In some Bible stories, God spoke softly to people. In others, He did amazing miracles. He parted a sea. He toppled a giant. He sent an angel.

"Another God adventure, please!" Sammy would say each time his dad would finish.

And after several stories, Dad even let Sammy stay up to read a few more.

When Sammy finished reading, he grabbed his sketchpad. Peering over the paper to look at his frog, Nile, he asked, "Now, how exactly do I draw a God who's big and strong but kind and gentle?"

"Ribbit . . ."

Joshua Loves God! Exodus 33:7-11

MOSE'S TENT

Looking for God:
Sammy loves Bible stories. His favorite one is about Samuel who heard God talking to him when he was just a boy. What are your favorite Bible stories?

4

Finding Frogs:
Sammy loves frogs because God used them to send Pharaoh a message. There are frogs everywhere in this book. Can you find them all, even the hidden ones? Have fun!

Looking for God:
Sometimes God reminds us in our hearts
of what the Bible teaches (John 14:26).
What is God saying to Sammy?

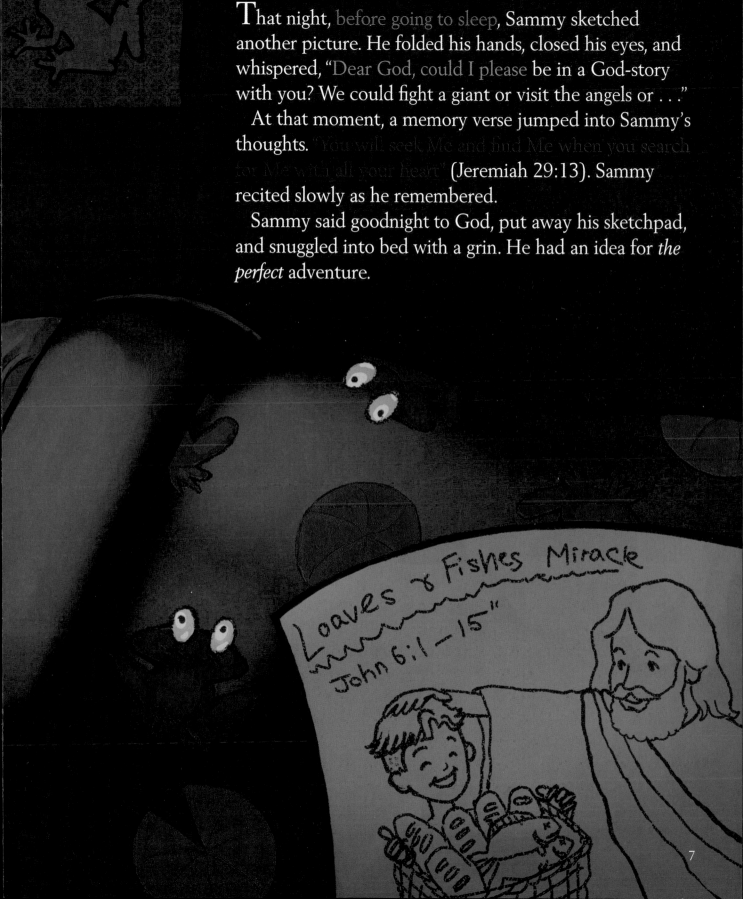

That night, before going to sleep, Sammy sketched another picture. He folded his hands, closed his eyes, and whispered, "Dear God, could I please be in a God-story with you? We could fight a giant or visit the angels or . . ."

At that moment, a memory verse jumped into Sammy's thoughts. "You will seek Me and find Me when you search for Me with all your heart" (Jeremiah 29:13). Sammy recited slowly as he remembered.

Sammy said goodnight to God, put away his sketchpad, and snuggled into bed with a grin. He had an idea for *the perfect* adventure.

Loaves & Fishes Miracle
John 6:1–15"

Sammy whistled all the way to breakfast, just imagining his incredible adventure. He bounced into the kitchen and pounced everyone with a hug before sitting down to eat.

"Hey Dad, can we go camping?" he asked between bites of peanut-butter toast.

"Sure, Sammy! You know I love camping," Dad exclaimed.

"This is sudden," Mom said with raised eyebrows.

"I want to go meet up with God," Sammy explained.

"Ohh, okay," Dad answered, glancing at Mom. "Well, Sammy, let's get our camping gear!"

Looking for God:
Who is God using now to help Sammy with his God adventure?
(Ephesians 6:1–4)

Jesus Age 12

Luke 2:41 - 52"

Dad picked the perfect spot to pitch the tent. But Sammy pointed at a rocky spot by the fire.

"Can I sleep out here, Dad?" Sammy asked. "It's part of my adventure."

"I-I guess so," Dad said a little puzzled.

"Yes!" Sammy shouted, giving the air a fist pump.

Looking for God:
Can you imagine an angel that is helping Sammy with his adventure? (Hebrews 1:14)

Jacob's Dream
Genesis 28:10-21

Sammy munched chocolate-peanut-butter smores as Dad read about Jacob's adventures with God. When it came time to sleep, Sammy found a flat rock for a pillow.

"I'll say prayers on my own tonight, okay Dad?"

"Okay, Sammy," Dad said as he curled up on the other side of the fire.

A chorus of frogs sang them both to sleep. "Ribbit, RIBBIT, rIbBiT."

Back at home Sammy wasn't his normal Sammy self.

"You know, Sammy, God is everywhere," his dad said.

"I know," Sammy replied as he poked his peanut-butter-and-dill-pickle sandwich.

"I'm going out for my hike today," Mom offered cheerfully. That gave Sammy an idea.

"Mom, could I please come? And could we please, please go up the mountain?"

"The mountain? Um, sure . . . if you want to," Mom answered.

"Thanks! I'll take my PB&P sandwich with me!" Sammy said, racing off to get ready. Mom looked over to Dad. He just shrugged.

> *Looking for God:*
> One way that God makes Himself real to us is by putting His wisdom in our hearts when we need it and trust Him for it (James 1:5). Do you think that God is helping Sammy with ideas?

King David – Psalm 139:1–18

Looking for God:
God shows us that He's at work in our lives by providing the things that we need (Genesis 22:13–14). Can you guess what Sammy needed for this mountaintop adventure?

Moses meets God
— Exodus 3

14

Even though Mom went for hikes all the time, she had trouble keeping up with the crunch, crunch, crunch of Sammy's shoes. When the path ended near the top of the rugged peak, Mom plunked herself down on a boulder to rest.

"Could I go up there?" Sammy asked pointing at a small, single bush.

"Sure," Mom said between breaths, "but climb carefully."

Sammy made his way up to the little bush, took his hiking boots off, and stood there, staring at it. After a while, Mom called him down to the path. Sammy walked back slowly, turning back to look at the bush every few steps, just to be sure.

"Sammy," Mom said, lifting his chin, "you know God hears you no matter where you are, right?"

"Yes, I know," he sighed.

Looking for God:
We experience God when He answers our prayers. What did Sammy say that he would ask and trust God for? (James 5:16–17)

Elijah Prays For Rain
—1 Kings 18:41–46

16

The next day, Sammy decided to try one more time. "Mom, could I sleep in the backyard tonight?"

"Not alone," Mom said. "And it's supposed to rain."

"I know! It's part of my adventure. I can pray for no rain like Elijah did."

"Adventure?" Sammy's older brother Ryan asked entering the room.

"I'll sleep outside with Sammy-bro-bammy so he can have his adventure."

"Thanks Ryan!" Sammy gave his brother's belly a hug. "And will you read God stories with me?"

"Sure," Ryan knock-knocked on Sammy's head, "anything to help you get your happy back!"

It was an amazingly clear night. Under the stars, Sammy and Ryan read
stories about God and Abraham. Ryan and Sammy counted shooting stars.
Ryan pointed out the North Star and the Big Dipper. After a while, Ryan
rolled over to sleep, and Sammy prayed while he stared at the stars.
Finally, he wiped away a tear and lay down. He was almost asleep,
when he thought he heard Ryan whisper, "I love you, Sammy."

"I love you too, Ryan!" Sammy whispered back.

"Ribbit, RIBBIT."

Looking for God:
The apostle Paul tells us that everyone can see and experience God by looking at His
amazing creation (Romans 1:19–20). How is God showing Himself to Sammy? Can you find
these things: shooting stars, the Big Dipper, the North Star, the Milky Way, and Saturn?

Dad had waffles stacked high when Sammy and Ryan came in the next morning. "How did it go?" Dad asked.

"Amazing!" Ryan answered, reaching for a plate. They were having peanut butter and bacon on waffles, the boys' absolute favorite. Sammy crossed his arms on the table and buried his head. Mom looked at Dad concerned.

Rrrriiiinng, rrriiinnnggg. Mom followed the sound and returned a few minutes later. "Sammy, Grandpa Henry would like to take you fishing." Sammy looked up. *Fishing? Maybe that will work!* he thought.

Looking for God:
Sometimes God shows us His love by inspiring people to do loving things for us (Galatians 5:22–23). Sammy loves peanut butter with just about anything. Who and what is God using to encourage Sammy?

Looking for God:
One of the ways we can experience God in our lives is by seeking out and listening to godly, wise people (Proverbs 12:15). What should Sammy do?

As Grandpa put the boat in the water, the frog chorus paused to listen. "So, your mom told me that you've been on a God adventure," Grandpa Henry said as he began to row. Splash, swish, splash, swish.

"Yes, Grandpa. But I don't think it's working," Sammy said without looking up.

"Maybe, I can help," Grandpa offered. Sammy was quiet. "Let me see," Grandpa continued, "camping with a rock for a pillow? That reminds me of the story of Jacob's dream. And standing shoeless in front of a bush sounds like Moses and the burning bush. A night under the stars is kind of like when God spoke to Abraham. And fishing—could be Jesus and the disciples? Am I right?"

Sammy couldn't hold it in anymore. He broke into tears and told his Grandpa everything. "I love all the stories about God, Grandpa." Sammy sniffed. "But they all show God coming and meeting with people and doing cool stuff. I know God loves me and hears my prayers no matter where I am but I wanted to—I don't know."

Grandpa put his hand on Sammy's shoulder. "You want to experience God like those people in the stories did?" Grandpa asked softly. Sammy nodded.

"Me too," Grandpa said with a smile.

Come to me
-Matthew 11:28-30

Looking for God:
One way we experience God is by feeling Him help us and teach us through difficult times (James 1:2–4). How is God helping Sammy right now?

"Here's the secret, Sammy," Grandpa explained. "We don't need to talk God into showing up. He's the One who has been working so hard to bring us to Him in the first place. "Really?" Sammy asked. "Yes!" Grandpa said nodding. "God was with you on every step of your adventure. He reminded you of your memory verse in Jeremiah. He used Bible stories to put each adventure idea in your heart. He gave you a family to help you with each adventure, and He even answered your prayers for a starry night. When you became a Christian, you became His son, and now you get to experience Him in new adventures every day."

Looking for God:
It seems that God has been using nature to talk to Sammy. A sunny day for fishing—and have you ever seen so many frogs? Using Sammy's drawings on the previous pages, can you find each different type of frog?

"God is happy that you're seeking Him, Sammy. I know it." Sammy looked up at his grandfather. "But how come I didn't get it, Grandpa?" Sammy asked quietly.

"You know, recognizing and obeying God takes a lot of faith and practice," Grandpa explained. "You've always liked drawing, but your pictures are much better now than when you first started." Sammy nodded. "Abraham, Jacob, Moses, and even the disciples all had to learn as well. God asked each one of them to believe in Him, trust Him, and obey everything He asked them to do. As you learn to do the same, you'll experience God more and more."

Sammy thought about that for a minute. "Grandpa, I think God is using you to talk to me right now!" Grandpa laughed and grabbed Sammy into a big hug. "Now, you're getting it!" he said.

"Grandpa?"

"Yes, Sammy?"

"Let's do some fishing."

Ribbit, RIBBIT, rIbBiT.

Sammy came flying in the front door. "Our Sammy is back!" Mom said laughing.

"I take it you had a good time?" Dad said tickling his way out of Sammy's belly hug.

"*Amazing!*" Sammy announced. We talked about God, caught a big bass, and saw a zillion frogs!"

Sammy hugged Ryan. "And Ryan, while we were camping, thanks for waking up long enough to tell me that you loved me. That really helped," Sammy said.

"Uh, Sammy-bro-bammy, I love you huge, but I was asleep the second my head hit the pillow. I didn't say that," Ryan confessed.

Sammy stopped for a second and looked confused. Then, in his heart, he remembered the Bible story about the other Sammy who heard from God. Sammy looked up and with a happy tear in his eye said, "God, I love you too! A LOT!"

Looking for God: Is God asking you to do something? Will you have trust in Him and obey whatever He asks? Tell Him. God says that when you search for Him with all your heart, you will find Him (Jeremiah 29:13). Start looking today!

Parent Connection

This book was specifically written and designed to hold several layers of learning that will help you talk to your children about Experiencing God at their own level and advance from there. God doesn't want our kids to experience Him just in their heads but in their hearts and lives as well. That's a journey that can take time and guidance.

Once you've read the story, you can go back over it again and again. There are many little details to find, Bible stories to explore, and questions to ponder. Have fun and help your children as they try to understand God's ways and His will in their lives. Here are some ideas that will help you use this book's features:

Find the Message
You'll notice that some of the story's text is in different colors. Go through all of the pages from beginning to end, and help your children find and write down all of the red words in the same order as they appear in the book. Do the same thing for both the green and the purple words. Each set of colored words written in order holds a different secret message: the red words reveal God's Word, the green words contain a blessing, and the purple words are a fun food prayer!

Looking for God
You'll find this feature in the book on almost every spread. It will help you engage your child in conversation about the story and help them learn how to recognize God at work in their own lives as well. After you've been through the story, you may also want to look up the Bible references supplied to read and discuss those with your child.

Bible Stories and Conversation Starters
Keep a Bible or Bible storybook handy and use your child's curiosity about Sammy's sketches to jump into a Bible story and conversation. Each sketch pictures a Bible story that correlates with the storyline on that spread and what Sammy is learning. Bouncing off into these stories when your child is curious will help your kids learn alongside Sammy. When reading from a full text Bible, you may want to use your own words to tell the story or have your child retell it in his or her own words.

Pages 4 and 5: Bible Story: Joshua Loves God, Exodus 33:7–11
Conversation: As a young man Joshua loved God and spent time seeking Him. When we love someone we should want to be with them.

Pages 6 and 7: Bible Story: Loaves and Fishes Miracle, John 6:1–15
Conversation: God doesn't just have adventures with adults. He uses kids and young people as well. Can you imagine how wonderful this boy felt being part of Jesus' great miracle?

Pages 8 and 9: Bible Story: Twelve-Year-Old Jesus, Luke 2:41–52
Conversation: God used Mary and Joseph in Jesus' life. That's why even Jesus had to listen to, learn from, and obey His parents.

Pages 10 and 11: Bible Story: Jacob's Dream, Genesis 28:10–21
Conversation: God used his angels to show Jacob that God was with him. Sometimes He sends us messengers to guide us or to remind us that He's always at work around us.

Pages 12 and 13: Bible Story: King David, Psalm 139:1–18
Conversation: King David knew that God was with him no matter where he was. God is with you, in you, at work around you, and is quick to respond when you call upon Him.

Pages 14 and 15: Bible Story: Moses Meets God, Exodus 3
Conversation: God had a big job for Moses to do. God has things for you to do as well. He'll start by having you do small things, and when you obey what He puts in your heart and tells you in the Bible, He'll trust you with bigger adventures.

Pages 16 and 17: Bible Story: Elijah Prays for Rain, 1 Kings 18:41–46
Conversation: Elijah didn't just say a quick prayer—he persisted, because he knew God would answer, and God did. Tell your children about a time when you trusted God and were patient until He answered.

Pages 18 and 19: Bible Story: God Talks to Abraham, Genesis 15:1–6
Conversation: God used a starry sky to help Abraham understand how many descendants he would have because of God's promise. It's possible that God was also implying that if He could create all that beauty in the night sky, He could certainly fulfill His promises. Talk to your child about how God's creation shows how powerful and faithful He is.

Pages 20 and 21: Bible Story: Elijah Hears a Soft Whisper, 1 Kings 19:9–14
Conversation: In this story God shows Elijah that sometimes He does things big and noisy, but often He does them privately and quietly. Talk to your kids about how Sammy is getting disappointed because God isn't showing up the way He has done for others. We need to trust God and see all the quiet ways He shows up in our lives too.

Pages 22 and 23: Bible Story: Paul Helps Timothy, 1 Corinthians 4:17 (and generally 1 and 2 Timothy, written by Paul to instruct Timothy)
Conversation: Paul called Timothy his "son in the Lord." Paul wasn't really Timothy's dad, but Timothy listened to him like he was. Timothy became a successful, godly man just like Paul because he knew to listen when God spoke through godly people. Think about some of the godly and wise people God has placed around you.

Pages 24 and 25: Bible Story: Come to Me, Matthew 11:28–30
Conversation: Jesus came and died because we needed our sins forgiven, but also because we can't get to know and experience God on our own without His help. God comes to us and helps us learn and grow and experience Him just because He loves us. If it ever seems hard, just ask Jesus for help.

Pages 26 and 27: Bible Story: God Uses Frogs, Exodus 8:1–15
Conversation: God can use anything to speak to us. In this story He used frogs to send a message. Tell your kids about a time that God used circumstances to show you something that He wanted you to know.

Pages 28 and 29:
Conversation: Start talking to your child about how they can seek and experience God while you're having fun finding frogs.

Page 30: Bible Story: God Talks to Samuel, 1 Samuel 3
Conversation: When your children pray, have them pause to be quiet and listen after or during the prayers. They may not hear God talking, but God will put wisdom, answers, and peace in their hearts as they wait. Tell them that God is always saying, "I love you!"

About the Authors:

Dr. Tom Blackaby is the second son of best-selling author Dr. Henry Blackaby (*Experiencing God: Knowing and Doing the Will of God*). He holds a B.Educ., M.Div. BL, and D.Min. Tom has served as associate pastor of music/youth/education in four churches and seven years as senior pastor of North Sea Baptist Church in Stavanger, Norway. He currently serves as International Director for Blackaby Ministries International. Tom has authored or coauthored *The Man God Uses* (and *The Student God Uses* version), *Anointed to Be God's Servants: Lessons from the Life of Paul and His Companions*, *The Blackaby Study Bible*, *Encounters with God Daily Bible*, *The Family God Uses*, *Experiencing God's Love in the Church*, and *The Commands of Christ*. Tom and Kim have three great kids and currently live near Vancouver, Canada, where they actively serve in their local church.

Rick Osborne is a best-selling author and producer of many fun and exciting books and multi-media resources that help strengthen families in their faith. For more info, helpful family content, and giveaways and contests, connect with Rick online. Don't forget to check out Rick's best selling "The Singing Bible," a musical that teaches children their Bible in a fun, memorable way. Watch the short video at www.TheSingingBible.com or visit www.rick-osborne.com.

 @RickOsborne   /RickOsborneAuthor

About the Illustrator:

Isabella Kung was born and raised in Hong Kong, then moved to the United States to continue her education at the age of sixteen. After moving around and exploring this new world for a few years, she finally landed in San Francisco, where she graduated from the Academy of Art University with a BFA in traditional illustration. Her training has allowed her to harness her narrative skills and painting ability to bring her very own touch to the world of children's books. Isabella currently resides in San Francisco, painting full-time and teaching part-time, with her husband and two extremely cuddly, chubby cats.

God
Talks to
Abraham

-Genesis 15:1-6